GW00864352

ELYOT goes to EARTH

ELYOT goes to EARTH

Keadi-Ann Williams

gatekeeper press
Columbus, Ohio

The views and opinions expressed in this book are solely those of the author and do not reflect the views or opinions of Gatekeeper Press. Gatekeeper Press is not to be held responsible for and expressly disclaims responsibility of the content herein.

Elyot Goes To Earth

Published by Gatekeeper Press
2167 Stringtown Rd, Suite 109
Columbus, OH 43123-2989
www.GatekeeperPress.com

Copyright © 2021 by Keadi-Ann Williams

All rights reserved. Neither this book, nor any parts within it may be sold or reproduced in any form or by any electronic or mechanical means, including information storage and retrieval systems, without permission in writing from the author. The only exception is by a reviewer, who may quote short excerpts in a review.

The cover design and illustrations for this book are entirely the product of the author. Gatekeeper Press did not participate in and is not responsible for any aspect of these elements.

Library of Congress Control Number: 2021936549

ISBN (hardcover): 9781662912542
ISBN (paperback): 9781662912559
eISBN: 9781662912566

DEDICATION

Lord, thank you for carrying me though this life. I can do nothing without you. I am so grateful for the way you have paved the path for my dreams to come true.

Thank you to my parents, Maxine and Courtney Roach, I appreciate you both for all your sacrifices you have made. I may not be able to pay you back for everything you have done . . . however, I will live my life trying. It is because of you both that I try my best to become a better version of myself daily.

For my brothers, you can accomplish anything you put your mind to. Don't just survive in this life, truly live, and never stop dreaming. Nothing is impossible and always keep God first.

Thank you to Olivia, also known as Pineapple, my dear cousin, for always reminding me that you believe in anything I touch, and contributing to my dreams.

Thank you, Jermaine Brown, my friend & confidant, for believing in this story and contributing to my dreams.

Thank you, Nicole Coutrier, for your encouragement through the years to never give up on this story that came from my heart.

INTRODUCTION

On a planet named Europa, there is a boy named Elyot. He lives with his parents and his big sister Kaley. Elyot's best friend in the whole wide planet's name is Nik.

Humans and aliens live in peace. The Europans travel back and forth to Earth. Aliens of Europa have a living stretchable organism called E-Tu, which they use to view other worlds. One of Elyot's favorite things to watch is the Annual Kids' Science Fair held in Kingston, Jamaica. One day he dreams of entering one of his inventions and winning first place.

Elyot looks through his E-Tu to view a park in Red Hills, Kingston, while Nik and Kaley wait for their turns. Elyot notices a girl named Charlie. (Charlie is playing with her puppy, Seven.)

"What do you see?" Kaley asks.

"Is it my turn yet?" Nik says.

"One day, I'll go to Earth and have my chance to enter the Kingston Science Fair."

Kaley shakes her head. "Yeah, right! Mom and Dad will never allow it."

Nik is surprised. "Why not? Elyot, I believe you will go one day - just take me with you."

Elyot thinks about the girl the whole way home.

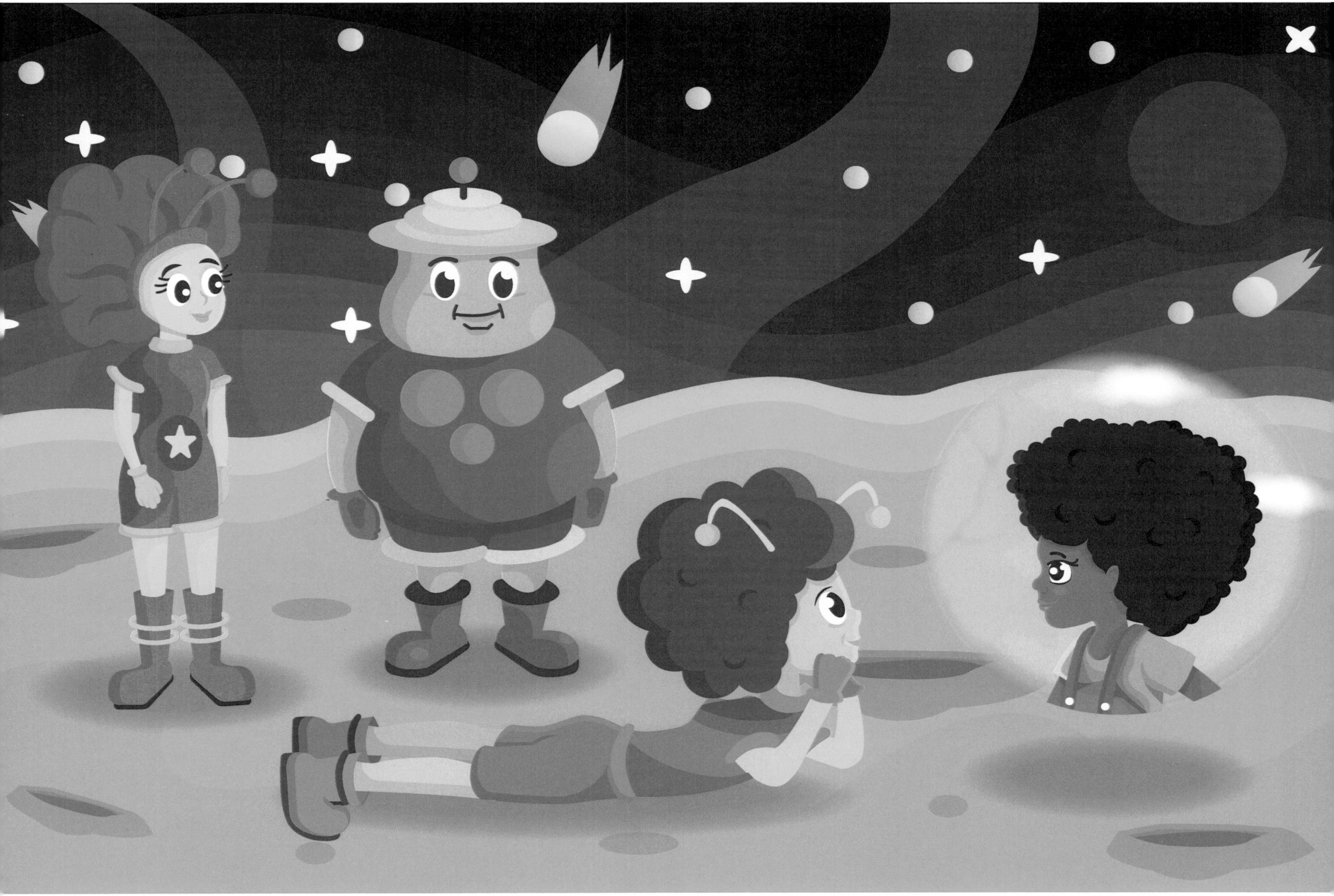

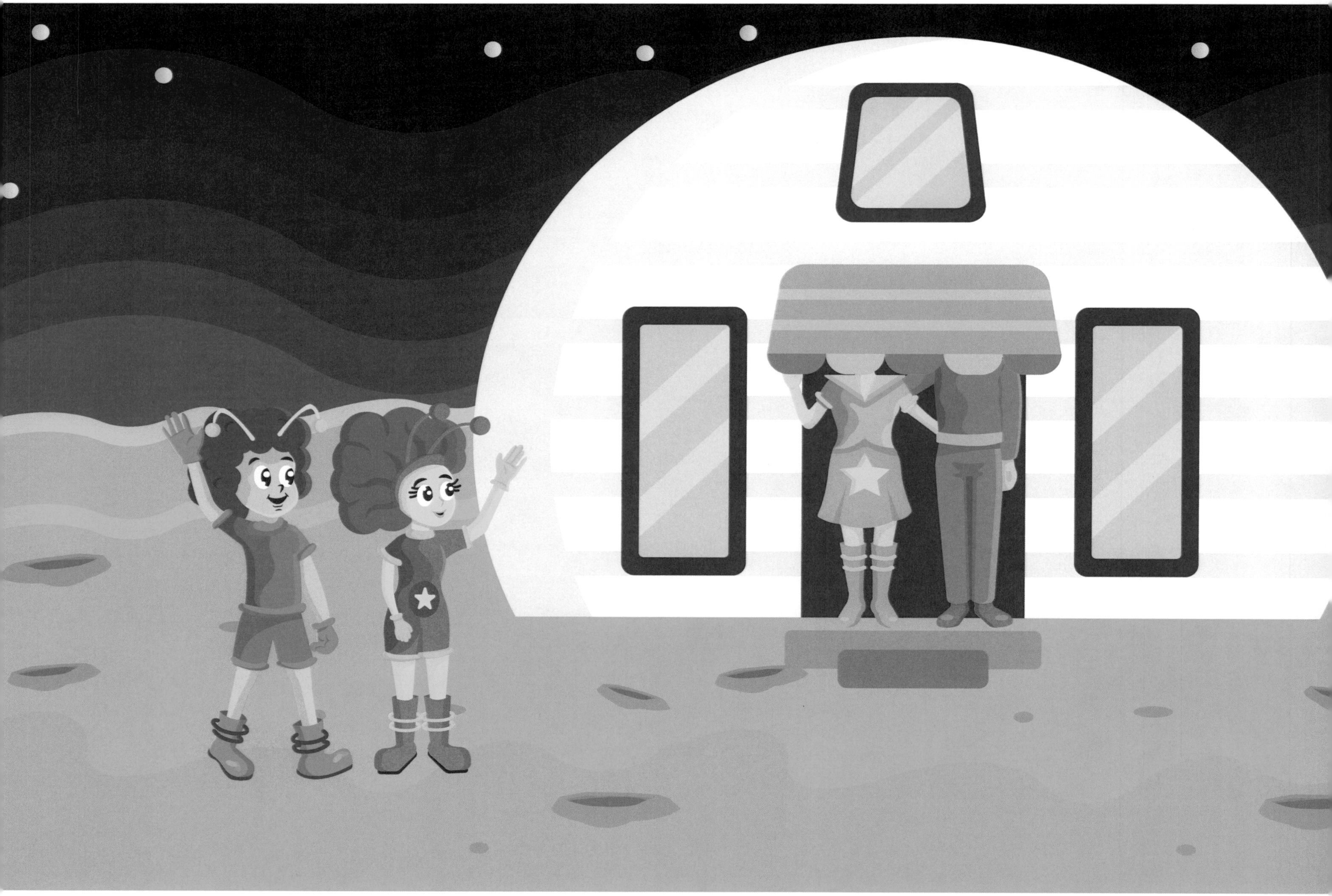

At the door Elyot and his sister are greeted by their parents. "Elyot! Kaley! What took you so long?" their mom asks.

"We were with Nik checking out the science fair. One day, I want to enter the contest. Mommmm ... can I? Can I, Mom? Pleaseeeee!"

"Maybe one day when you have proven yourself responsible and you are a bit older we will see," Dad says.

Elyot and Kaley are sent to bed. Elyot sneaks out of his room and hides behind a large metal couch to watch E-Tu with his parents. He is wishing and hoping that one day he will have his chance to go to Earth.

The next day, Elyot and Kaley meet up with Nik, and they decide to watch their favorite kids again. But Elyot only has eyes for Charlie. She often hangs out at a park in Red Hills, Kingston, called Hughenden. It is very popular amongst the local kids.

Charlie reminds Elyot of himself. She's not popular and she's a bit of a loner. She enters the local school science fair every year, although she never wins. Elyot feels a connection to Charlie. She has so much to offer but she's very shy. Other kids often pick on her because she is tall for her age and has huge hair.

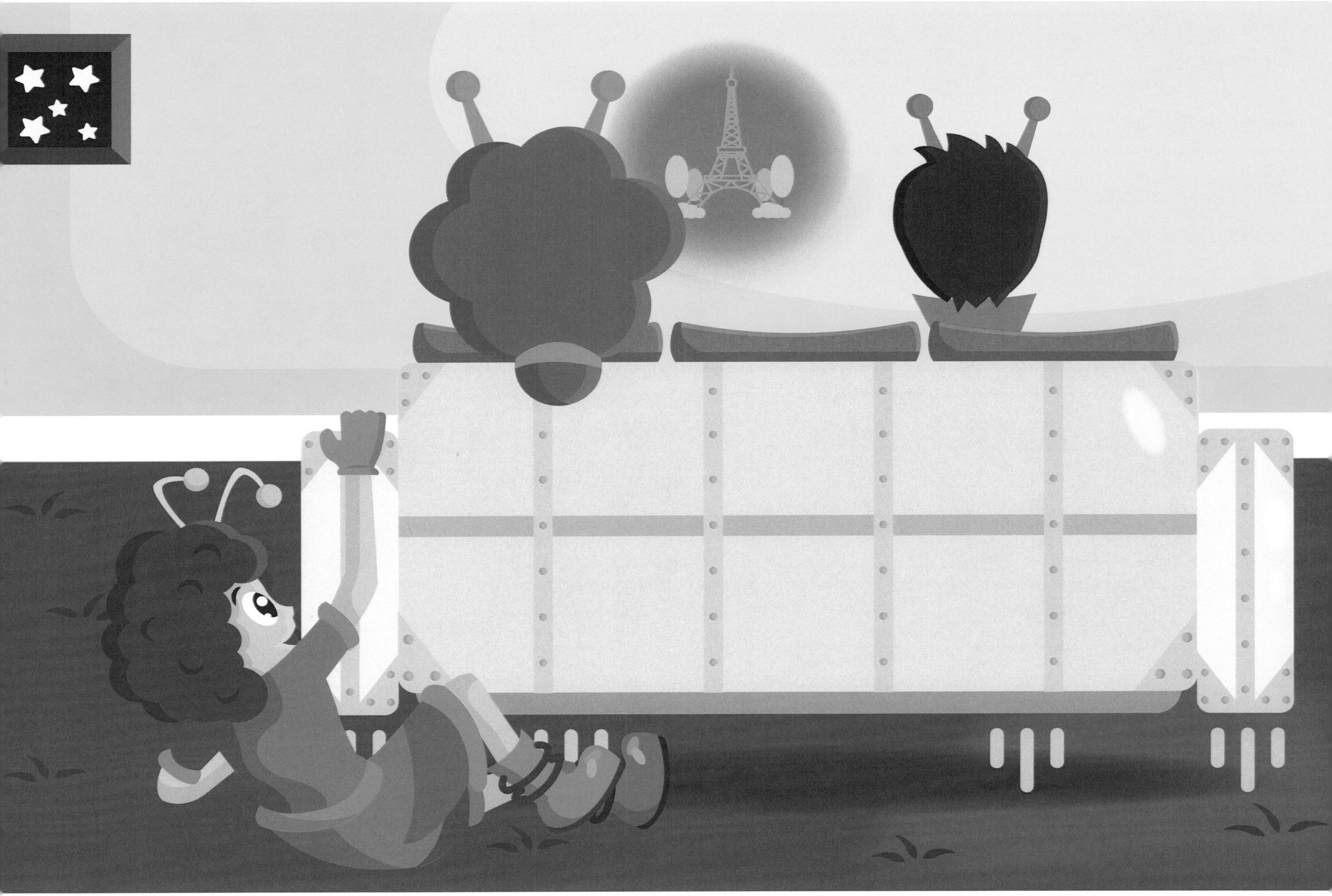

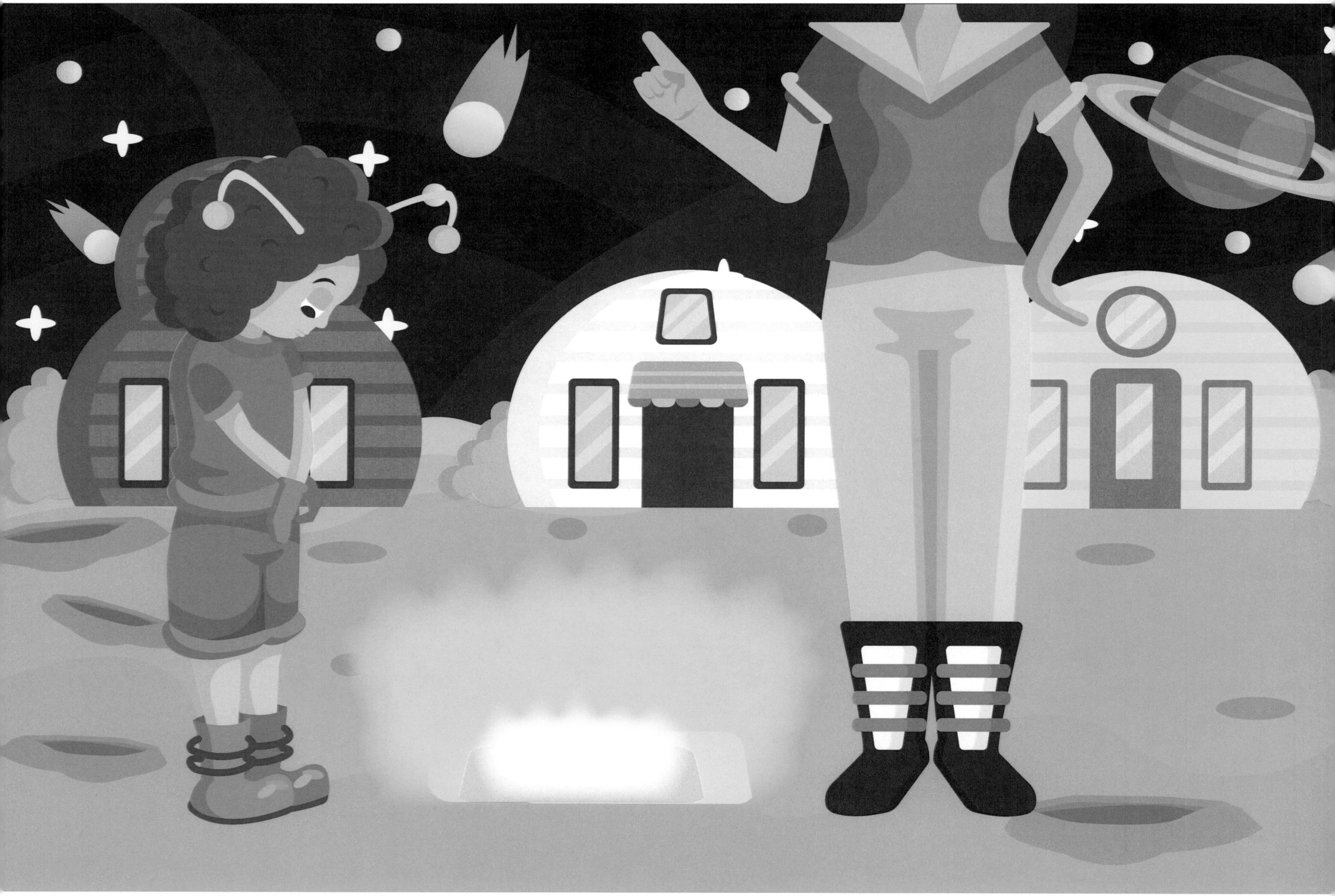

Europan citizens travel to Earth using a light portal that appears from the ground and whisks them to different locations around the world daily. Elyot often tries to sneak into the portal, but he never succeeds and always gets into trouble. This has made his parents very worried that they may not be able to trust him.

One day, a puppy runs through the portal while escaping a dogcatcher. Elyot is watching. He reaches into his bag and puts a globe on the puppy so that he can breathe.

Elyot has a new friend! He's excited. He decides to name him Nine. Many years ago, Elyot lost his pet to the portal and he was never the same. Nine renews his happiness.

Content with his new buddy, Elyot stops trying to sneak into the portal. He doesn't like the look of disappointment on his parents' faces after he disobeys them. He realizes that in order for him to truly get a chance to go to Earth, he will have to follow the rules. Elyot decides to rebuild trust again and prove himself. With his new pet and his dreams for the future, he decides to focus on creating a science project.

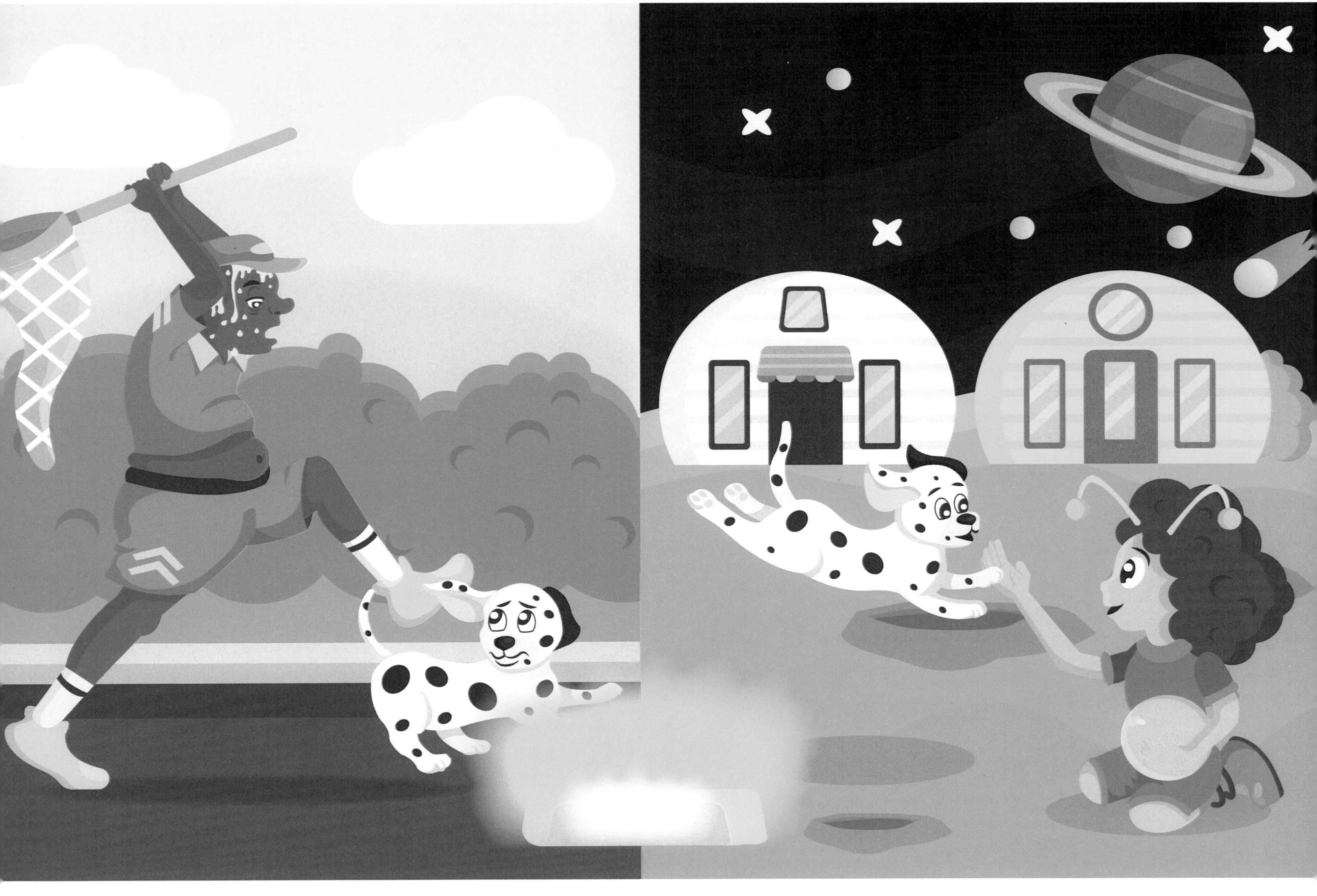

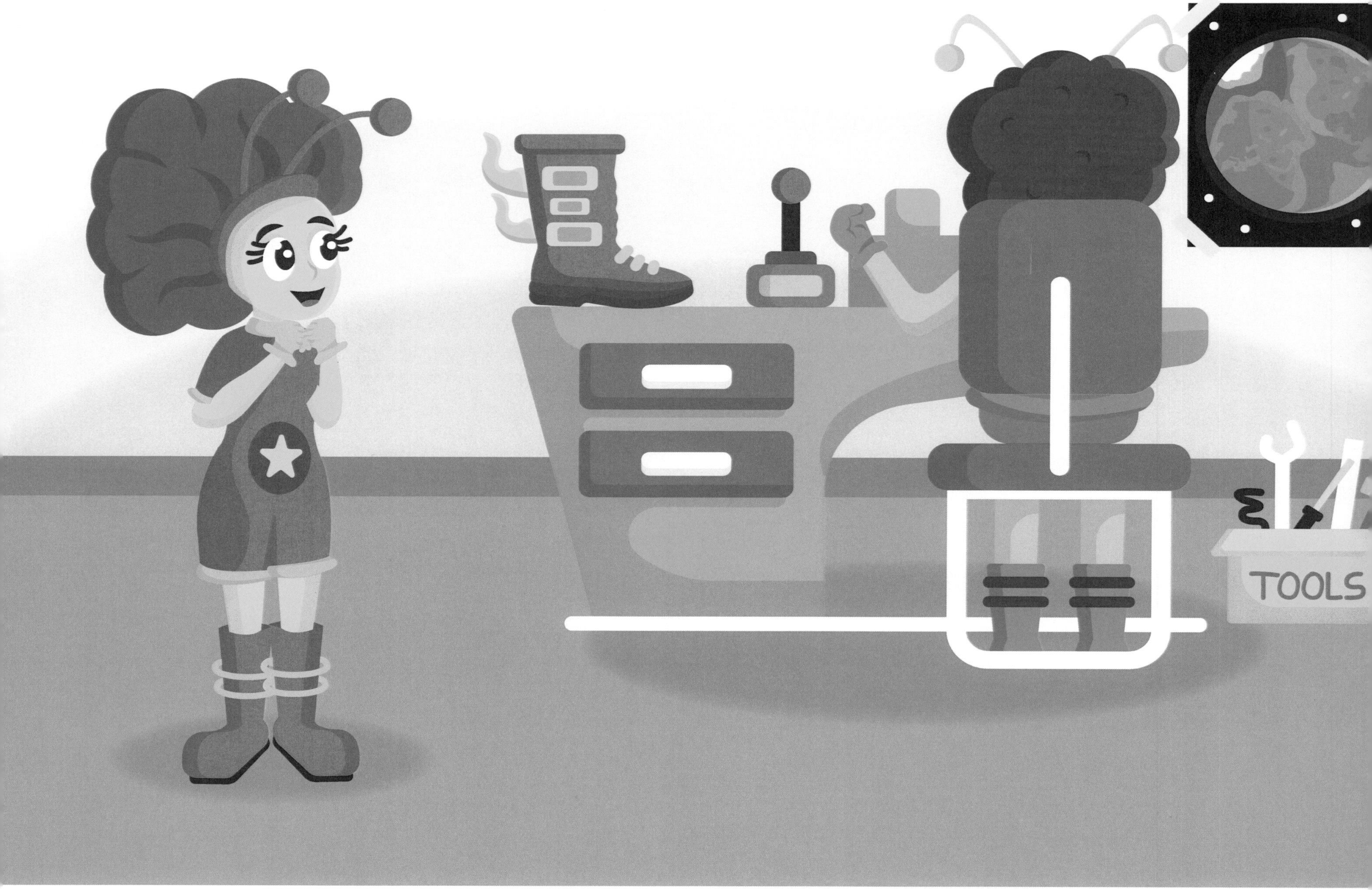
TOOLS

Elyot works hard in his room, inventing a set of boots that allow earthlings to walk normally in space and glide on Earth. Over the years, he's often seen humans struggle in space. They float and are unable to control their movements.

(Kaley peeks into Elyot's room and tiptoes in.)

"Elyot? Whatcha doing? You and Nine haven't been outside to play in forever! We want to play. Let's go outside!"

"Okay ... I'm coming, just one last touch. Thereeee ... that should do it. Okay, I'm ready ... let's go!"

Elyot, Kaley, and Nine go outside and meet up with Nik.

Elyot tells Nik and Kaley about his invention, and they both plead with him to try out his space boots.

Problem is, when they try on the boots they don't work because Elyot, Kaley, and Nik are from space and they walk normally. Nik and Kaley think Elyot's boots don't work. They think he should give up the idea and forget about going to Earth and entering the science fair. Elyot believes in his creation and intends to prove them wrong.

As time passes, Elyot's parents see how much he has improved with following all the rules. They tell Elyot that for his Eurpanday, which is his birthday, they will allow him to go to Earth for one day as his reward for being obedient. He chooses the day of the Kingston Science Fair contest.

Elyot is excited. He and Nine run off to tell Kaley and Nik the good news.

"Guys! I'm going to Earth for one day!"

Kaley answers, with big eyes, "Oh! No way!"

"Can we come?" Nik asks.

"You have to get permission, but I want you both to come with me," Elyot responds.

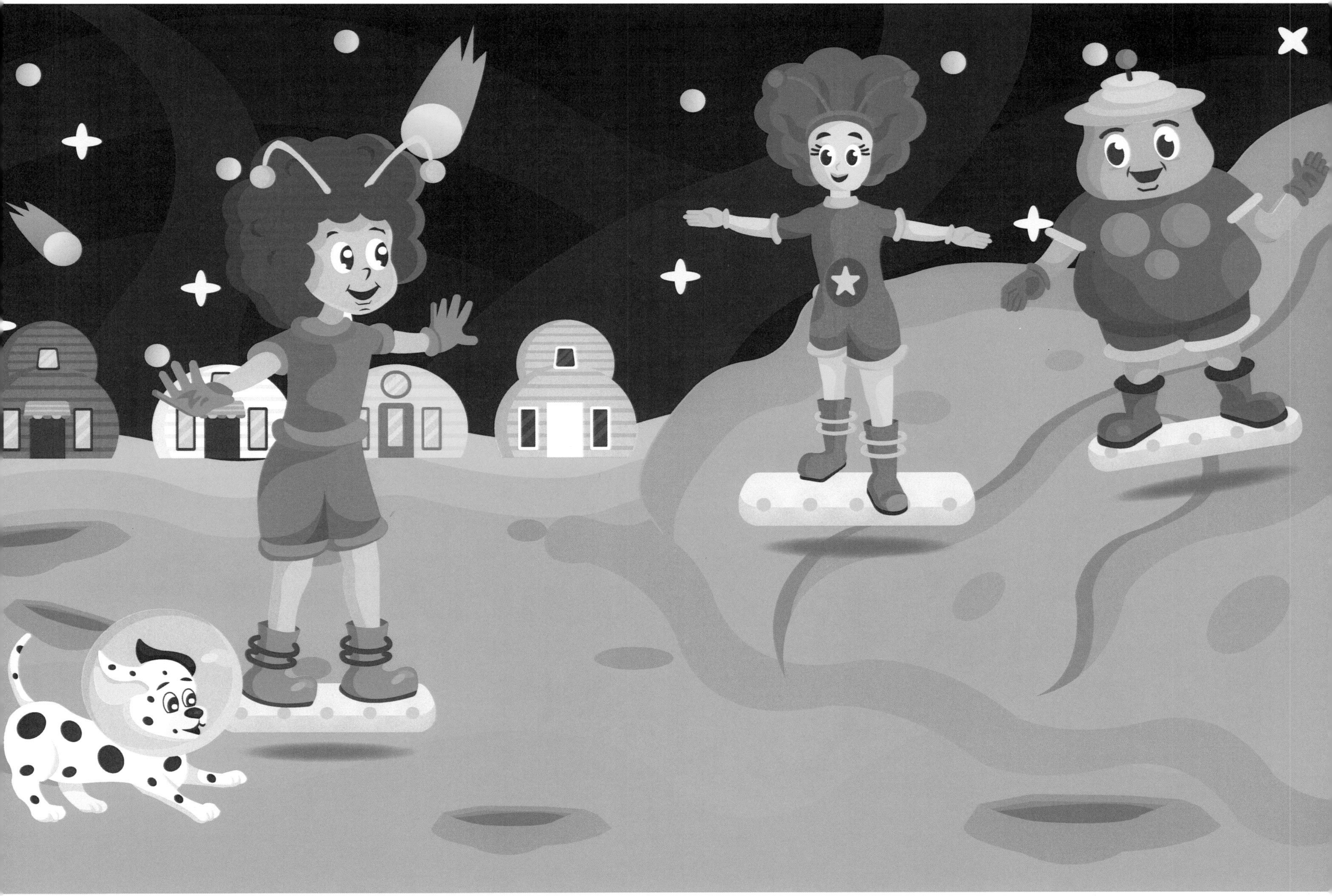

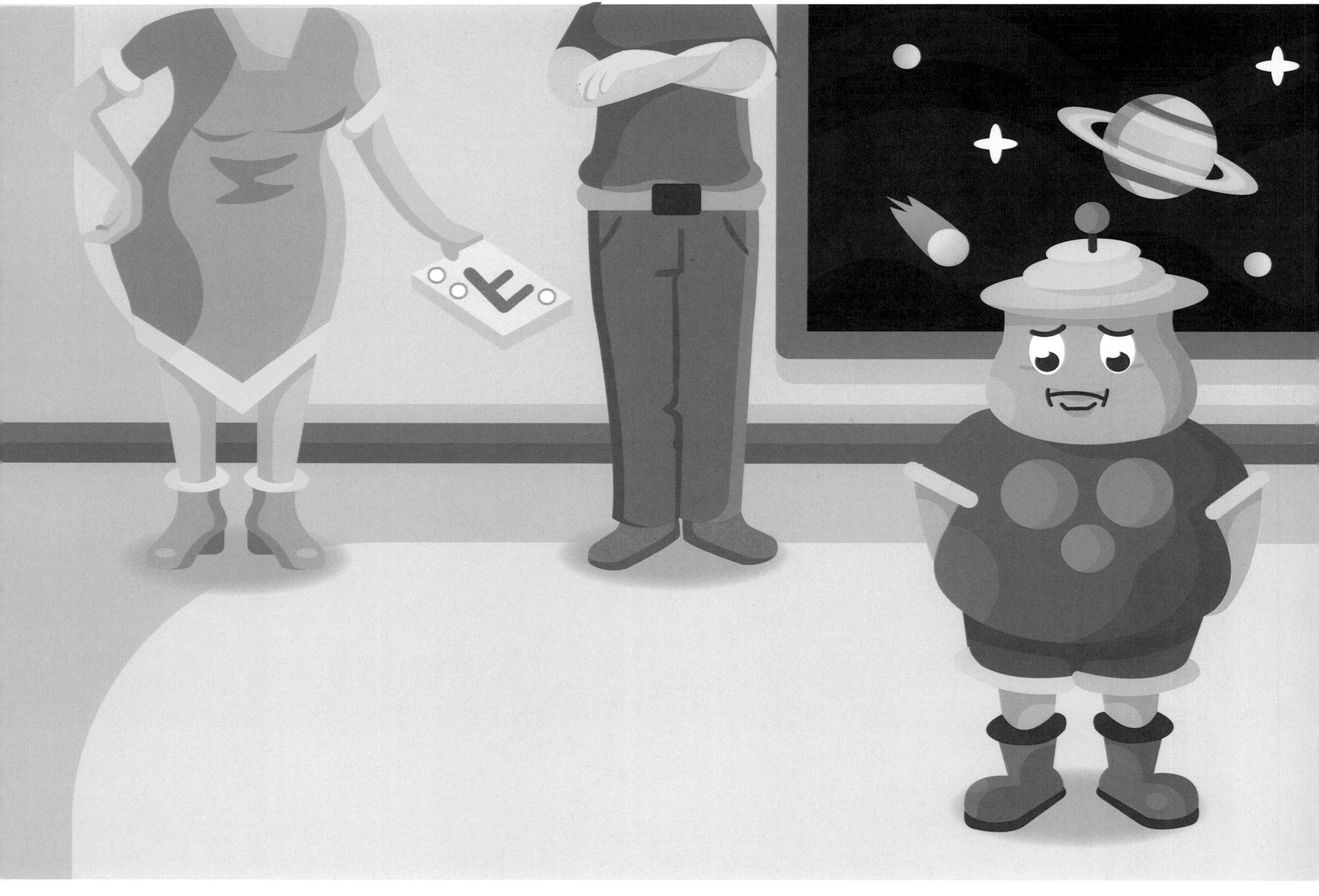

Elyot's parents think it's a good idea for his sister to go. This way they can protect each other.

Nik doesn't get permission from his parents because he did not do well in Europurpello, which is Europan school. But his parents agree to allow him to watch through E-Tu.

Elyot lays down, staring at the planet. He is a little scared, as he never had a chance to try out the space boots on Earth. He wonders, *will the boots work?*

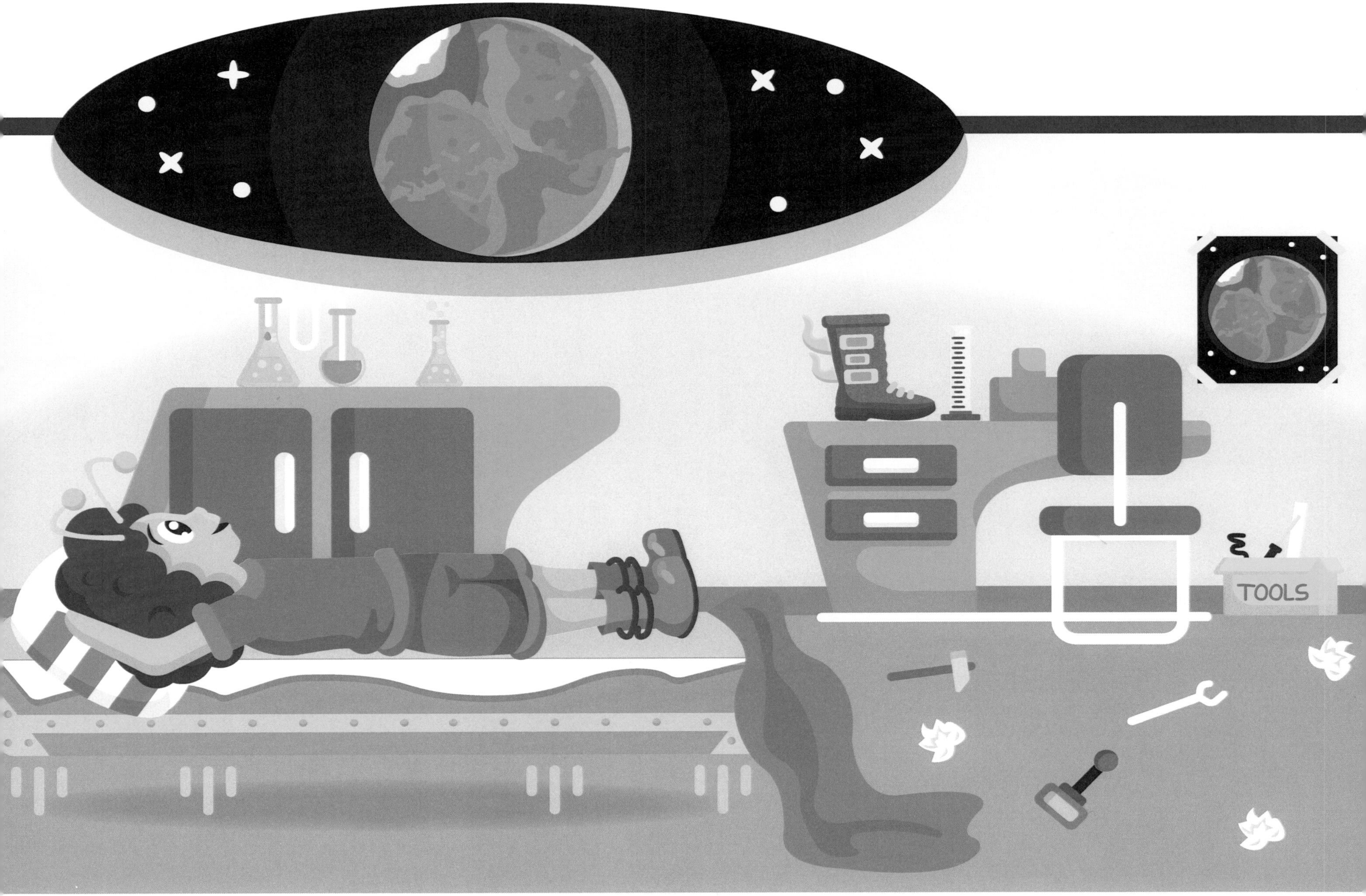
TOOLS

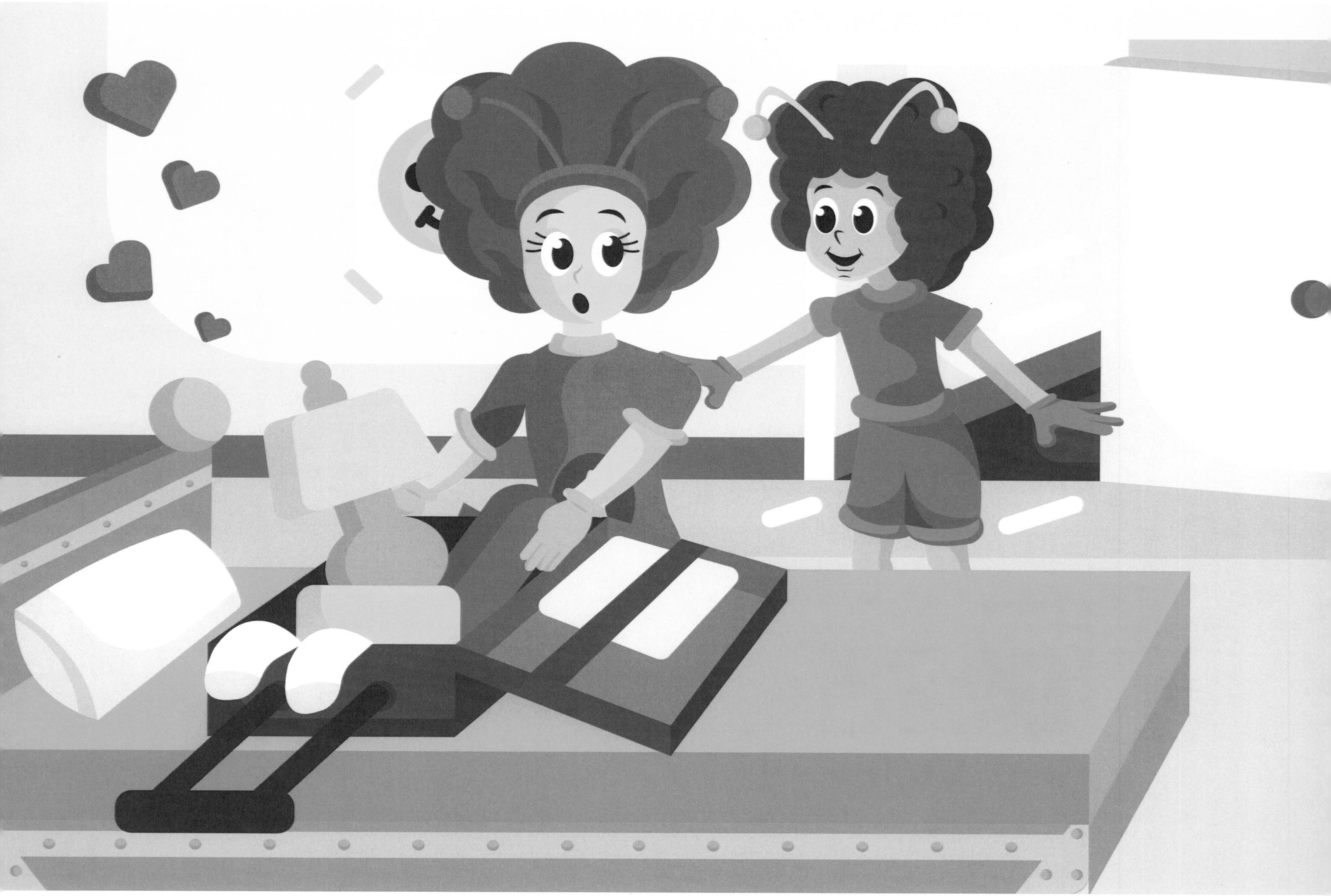

Elyot and Kaley count down the days and nights.

"How do you know they will work?" Kaley asks.
"It has to work Kaley ... it has to work!" Elyot responds.

The time for Elyot and Kaley to go to Earth finally arrives! Elyot wraps up his space boots carefully, and their parents take them to the portal and set the timer. Their parents explain that they must return to the portal in order to come back to Europa.

"Kaley, Kaley, come on! You're taking forever!"
"I don't want to leave anything!"

"You must be back in 24 hours," Dad says.

(A bright light that looks like a door emerges from the ground. Elyot and Kaley walk through it and appear in Hughenden Park.)

Some kids nearby are playing football. Elyot and Kaley keep looking at the kids and notice a little girl sitting on the other side on a bench with a pink dog with two ears and two tails. It's Charlie, the girl Elyot often watches.

Elyot is so anxious to see Charlie but wants to be careful before revealing himself to her.

"Charlie!" Kaley yells out.
(Elyot pulls his sister behind the bushes.)
"Kaley! No! What are you doing?"
"Let's go say hi! Charlie! Over here!" Kaley yells.

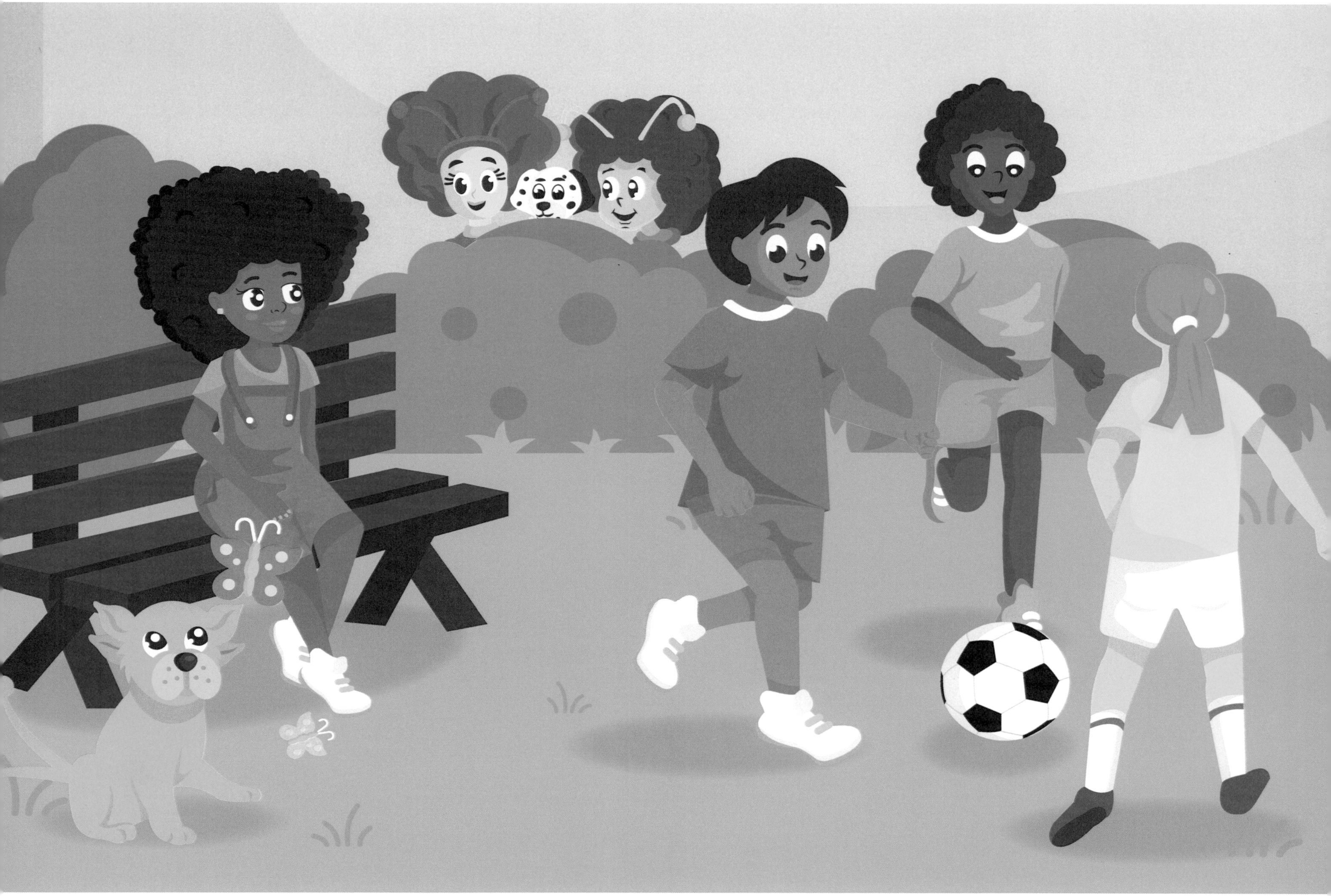

(She starts walking over to the bushes.)
Kaley and Elyot see Charlie coming, and Elyot grabs Kaley and hides.

Charlie looks over to the bushes and sees no one. She yells, "Who's there?"
"Us!" responds Kaley.
"Us, who?" Charlie asks.
"Don't be scared of us! We come in peaceee," Kaley giggles. Kaley pops out from the bushes and says, "Hi, Charlie!"
"Was it you calling me?" Charlie responds.
"Yes, my brother and I."
"Where is your brother?" Charlie asks.
Kaley pulls Elyot out of the bushes. "This is my brother, Elyot."
"Wapan, Elyot!" Charlie says.
"Wha agwan?" Elyot asks.

"Wait, you speak Patois? How do you know my name?"

"We know every language in the universe, and we have been watching you on E-tu for a very long time," Kaley tells her.

"E-tu, a wha dat?" Charlie asks.

"It's a way for us to see all countries from our planet," Kaley answers.

"Wow! That's amazing! So what are you guys doing here?"

"We are here to enter the science fair!" Elyot answers.

"No way!" Charlie responds.

They all decide to teach each other a little about their worlds. Elyot and Kaley show Charlie some really neat tricks.

Charlie introduces ice cream and gum to Elyot and Kaley. Kaley takes a special liking to gum and starts to chew it all the time.

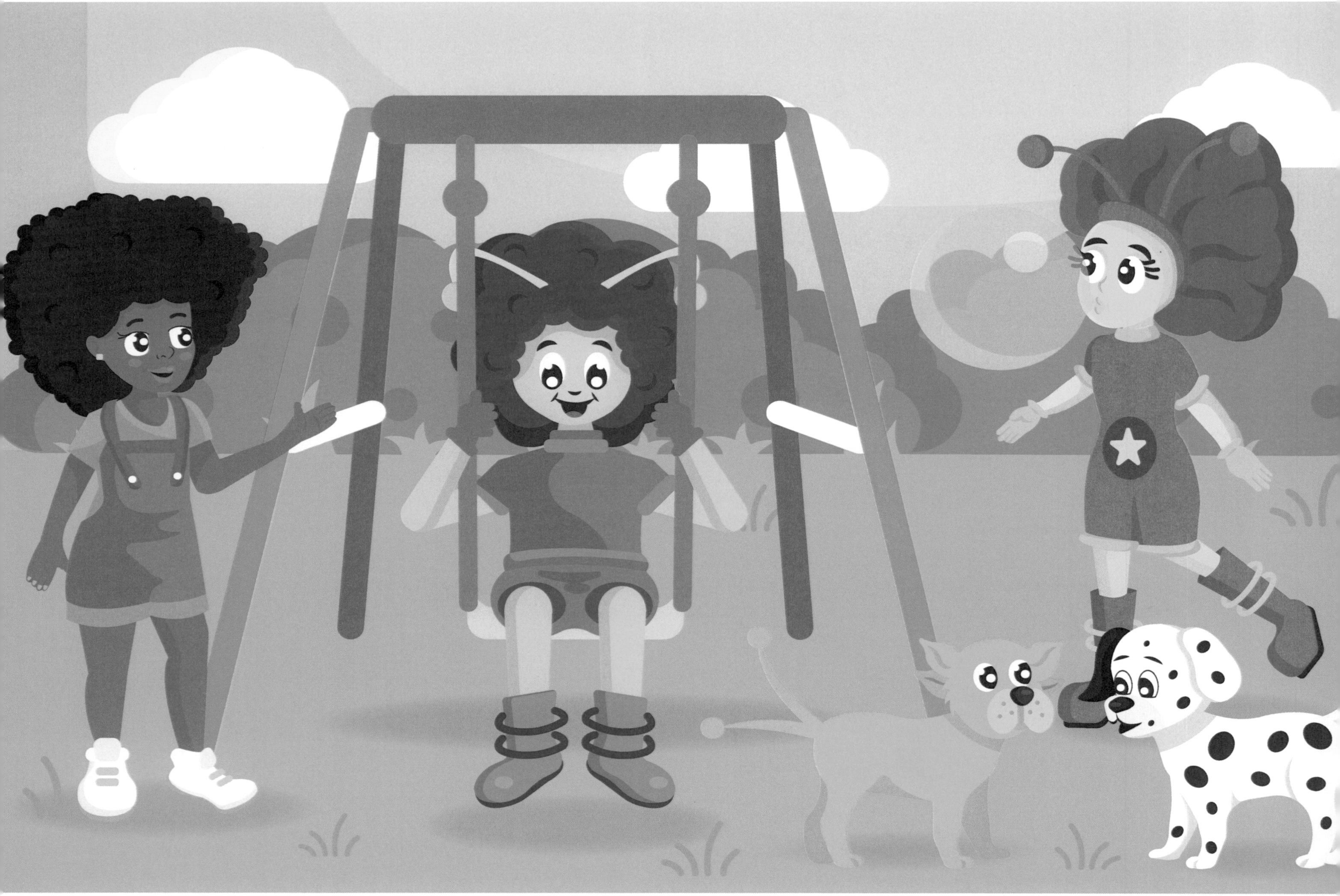

Charlie decides to take Kaley and Elyot to her home just beyond the park gates.

"So, Elyot, can I see your project?" Charlie asks.
"Sure! Are you entering this year?" Elyot says.
"No, I never win; I am not entering this year."

Elyot pulls his space boots out of his bag and tells her to put them on. Charlie tries on the boots and hits the red button and nothing happens. Elyot tries the button several times, over and over again, but still nothing.

Elyot plops down on the floor, feeling sad.
Kaley sees her brother and goes over to comfort him.

"Don't worry! We will figure it out!" Kaley cheerfully responds.
"We don't have time; the contest is tomorrow! I can't believe it's not working.
I must have missed something. We came all this way for nothing!" Elyot says.

Charlie takes the boots off and starts to closely examine them. She is sure they
can fix it but it will take time. Charlie and Elyot work all through the night.

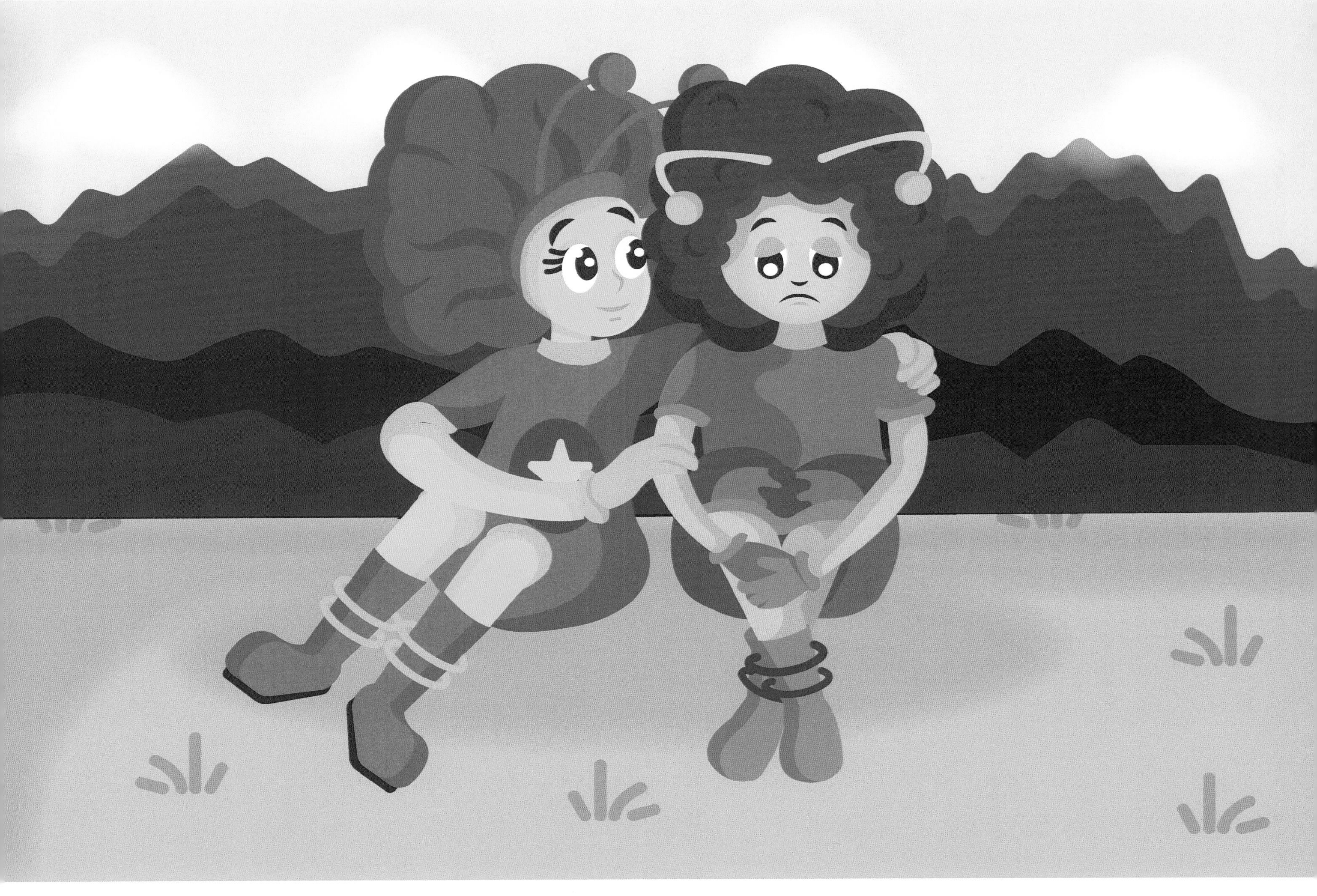

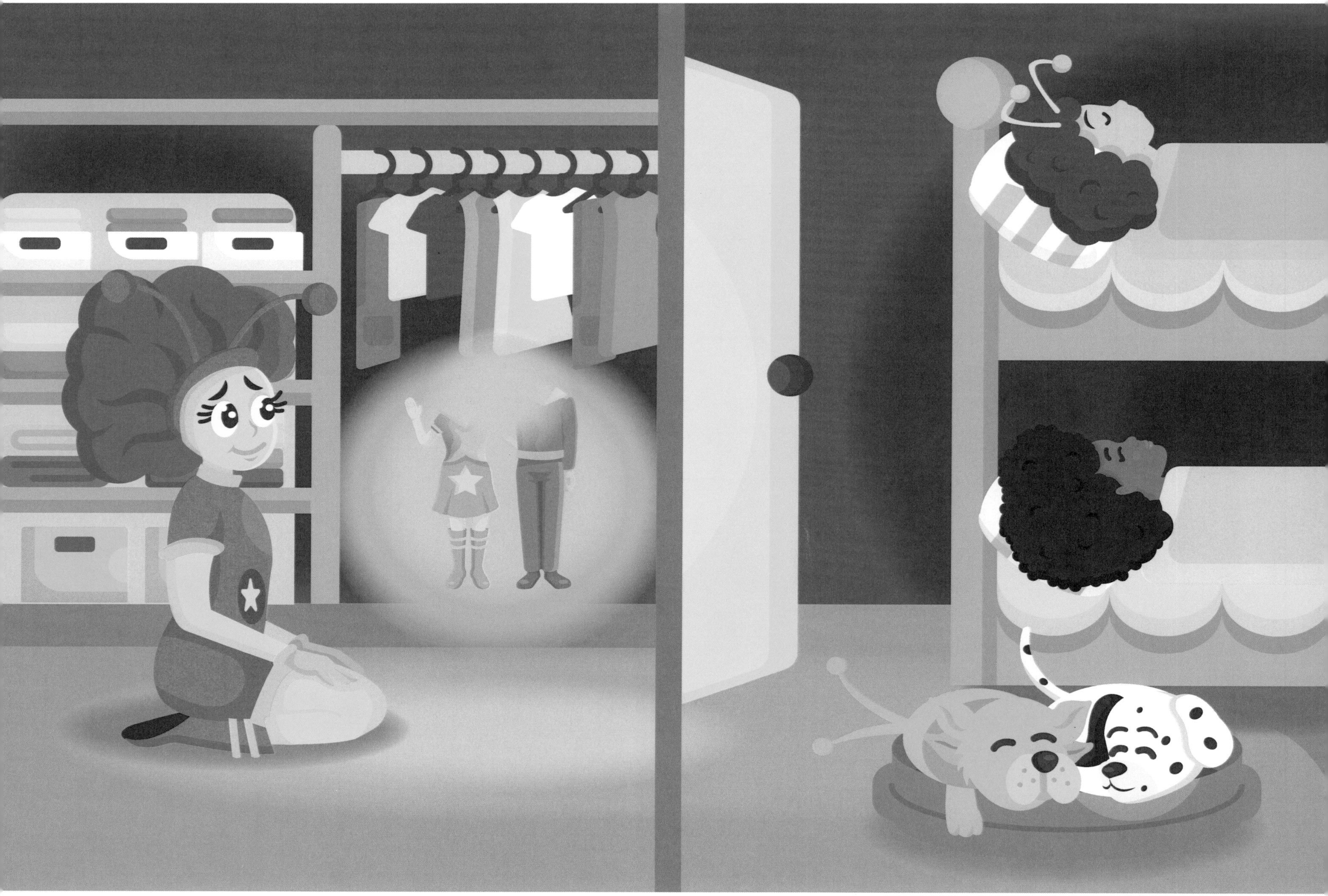

While everyone is finally sleeping, Kaley goes into a small closet nearby and activates her E-Tu. She wants to check on her parents. It is as if they are looking right back at her. She waves gently. She can go to sleep peacefully knowing they are okay.

(The sun rises.)
"Wake up! Wake up! Yayyyyyyyy, it's almost time!" Kaley shouts and runs toward Elyot.
"Charlie and Elyot, wake up!" she repeats.

Elyot and Charlie agree that since they worked on the boots as a team, they will enter the science fair together. They couldn't have completed it without each other.

Elyot, Kaley, Charlie, and their pets make their way to the Kingston Science Fair down on Halfway Tree Road. Kaley and Elyot are fascinated when they get there. Many kids entered their projects. They feel so nervous!

"We came so far. You guys will do great, and I am here to cheer you on," Kaley says.

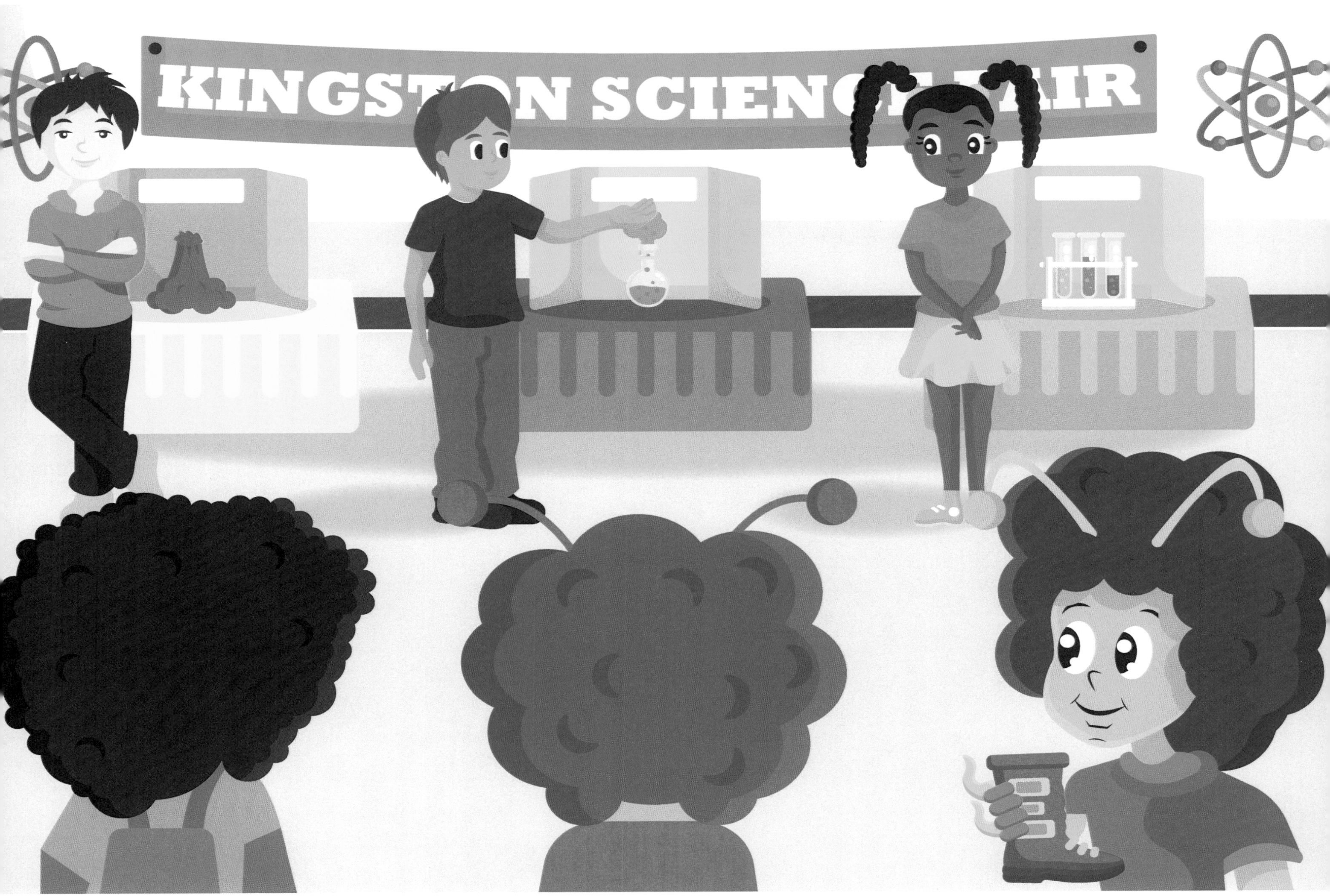

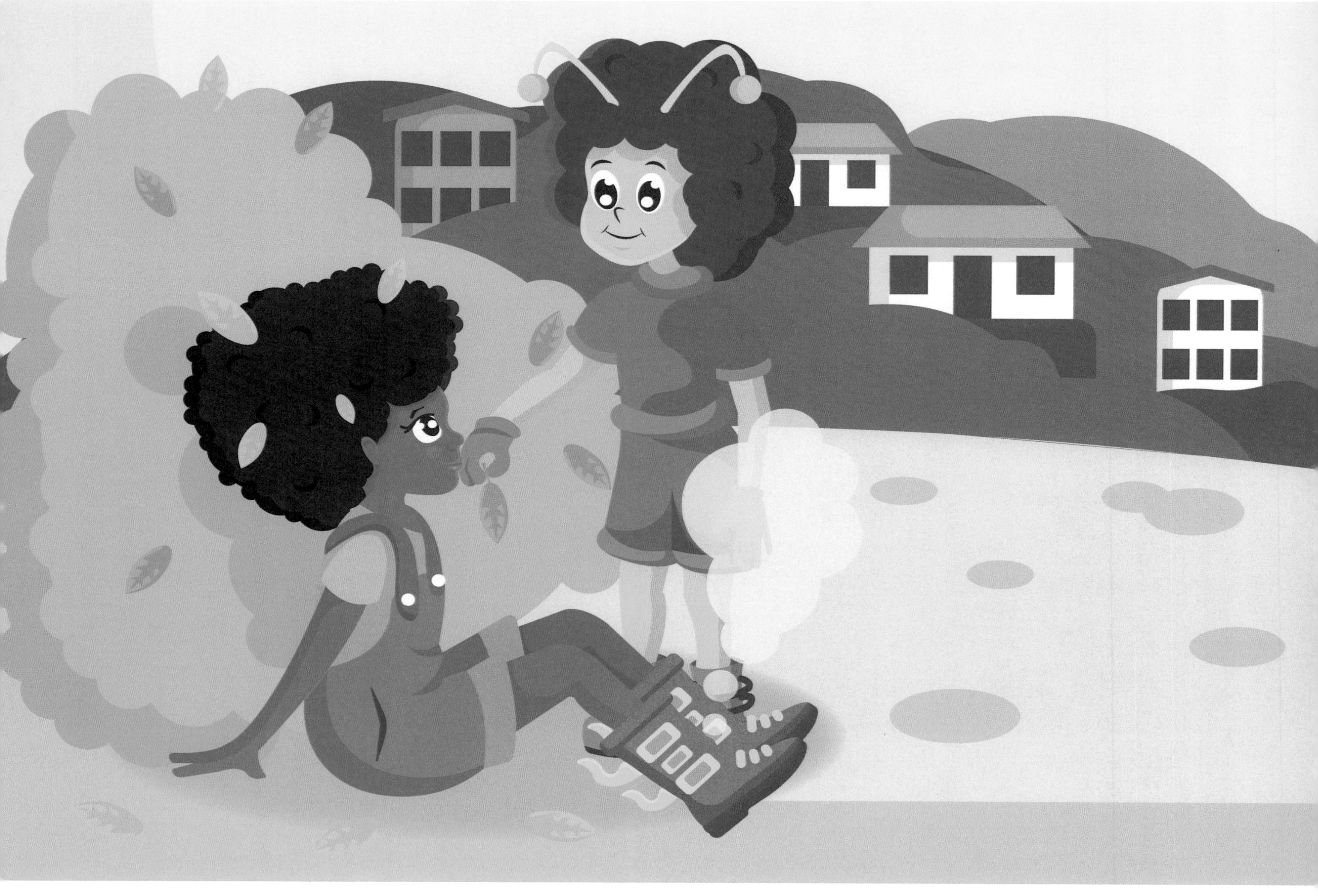

After they sign up, Charlie and Elyot decide to try out the boots before the contest begins. There is a nearby field that gives them enough privacy to do one last test run.

Charlie tries on the boots and Elyot hits the red button. The boots work and Charlie is flying! All of a sudden, the boots start to smoke and Charlie comes crashing down. Elyot runs over to make sure she is okay.
(Elyot removes the grass from Charlie's hair.)

"Mi alright man," Charlie says.
She thinks they must have missed something. They have a few hours before the contest begins, so they decide to work on the boots.

Back at the science fair, Kaley notices a small metal object. She doesn't know what it is for, but she thinks it is so unique that she decides to keep it.

Elyot and Charlie make their way back to the science fair and they meet up with Kaley. It is almost time for the contest. Kaley sees their faces and asks "What's wrong?" They explain that the boots worked for only a few minutes before shutting down.

They don't know what to do and they don't have enough time to figure out the problem. They are about to give up.

"Don't give up," Kaley says.

They are so scared and time is running out.

As the judges approach them to check out their invention, Kaley notices that the small, oddly-shaped piece of metal she found fits on the boots. She quickly puts it on and then smiles. She now feels officially included. Somehow she knew in her heart that this would fix the problem.

One of the judges asks with a stern voice, "All of you worked on this project?" They all say, "Yes."

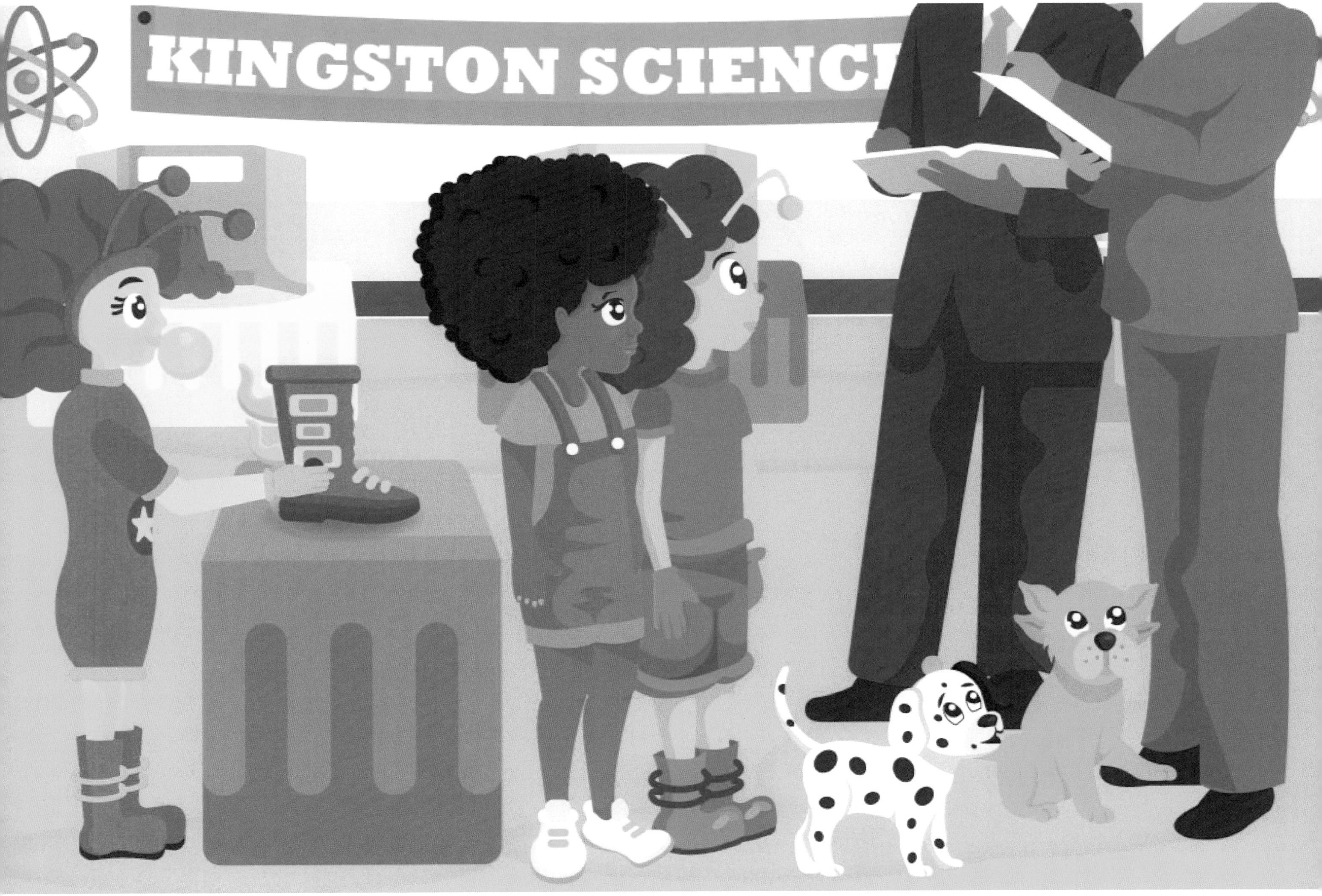
KINGSTON SCIENC

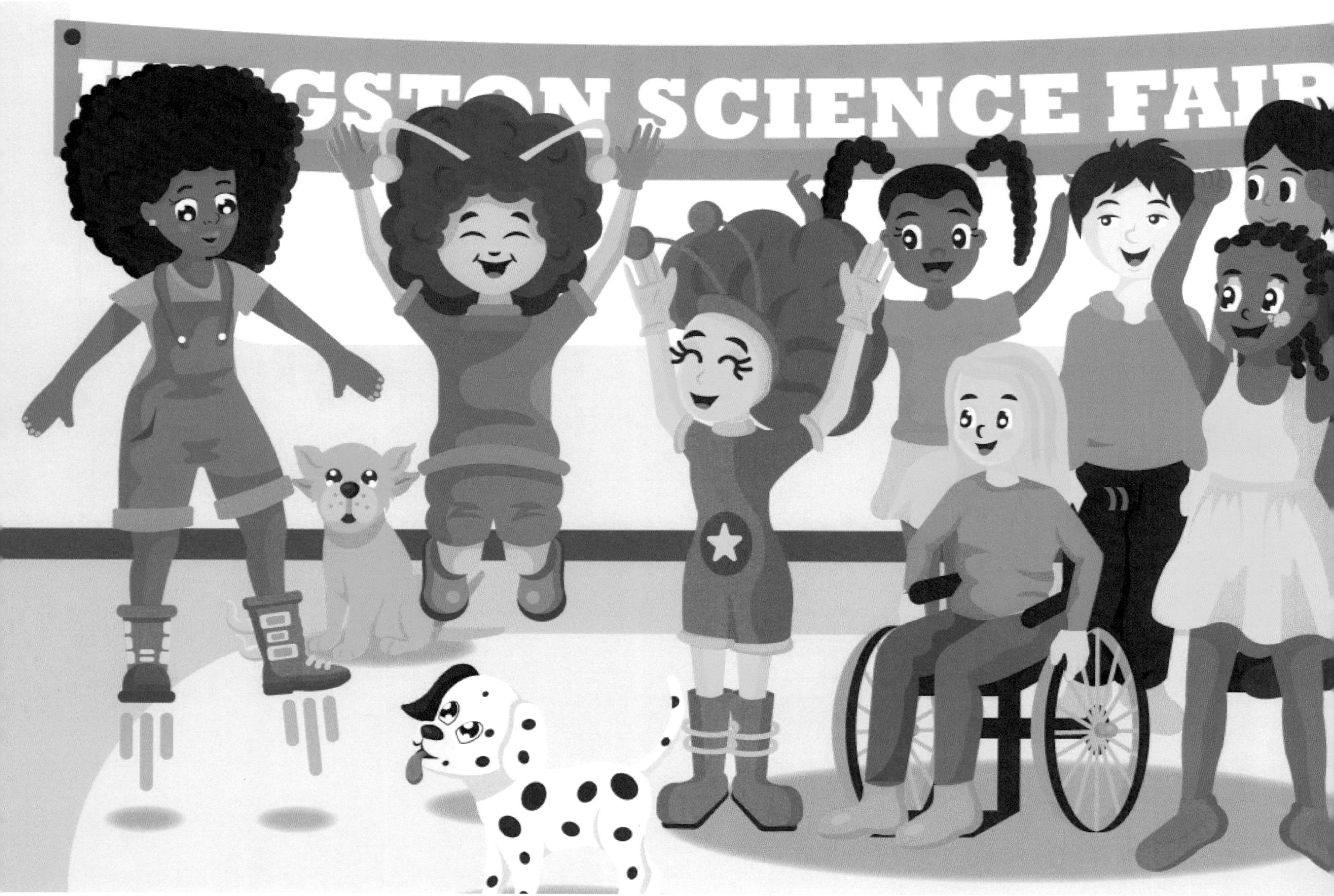
GSTON SCIENCE FAI

Charlie jumps in the boots. Elyot straps her in carefully and Kaley presses the red button. Charlie glides successfully!

The contest is not over yet. Elyot's reason for inventing the boots was to help humans walk normally in space as they do on Earth. So even though the boots glide on Earth, now the judges have to make sure that the boots work in outer space. One of the judges prepares Charlie for the portal. She is then beamed to Mars. Charlie starts to float. She is as light as a feather and amazed by the stars and the planets. Charlie clicks the button and begins to walk, then she takes off running. The boots work!

The judges are overjoyed, all the kids are amazed, and the dogs are so happy!

They are proud!

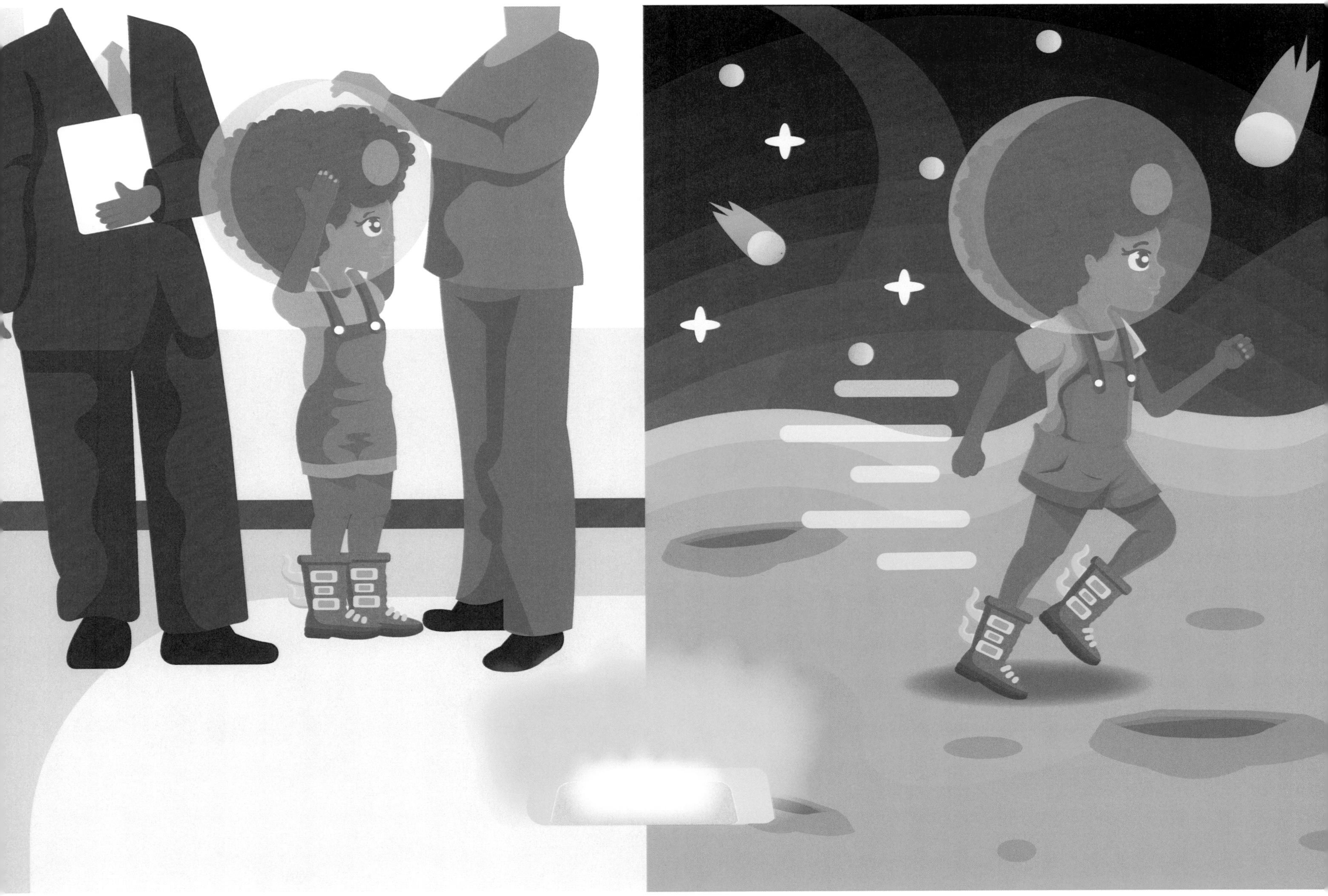

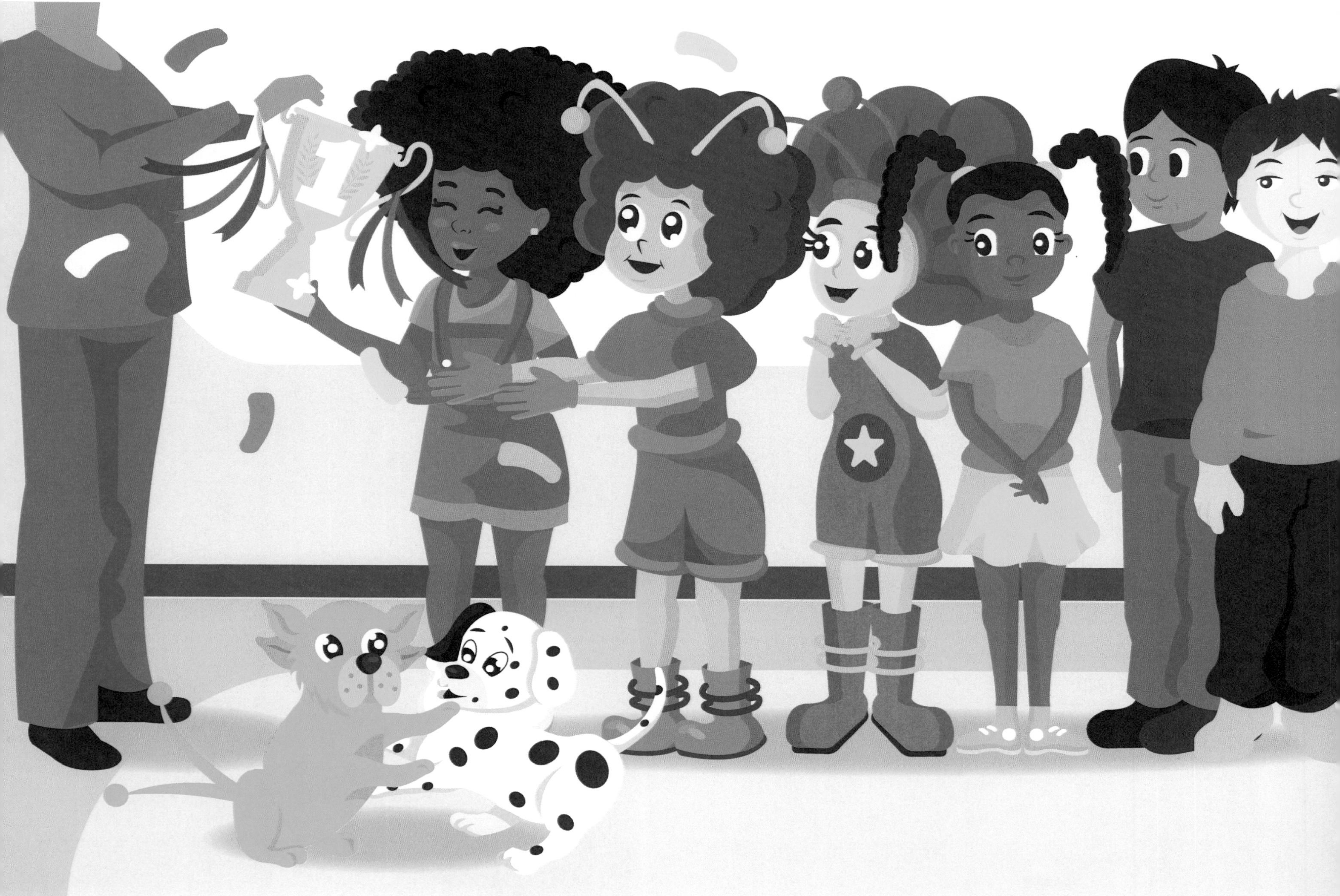

Even if they don't win, Elyot is happy to come to Earth, Kaley feels included in the contest, the dogs are fond of each other, and Charlie has gained some wonderful friends.

The judges make their decision. Elyot and Charlie, with the help of Kaley and the dogs, win first place in the Kingston Science Fair!

All of planet Europa, including Kaley and Charlie's parents, watch on E-Tu and cheer for their achievement!

Unfortunately, they notice that it is almost time to return home. Twenty-four hours are almost up. They run through Red Hills Road, pass Vilma Avenue, and jump through the park gate quickly.

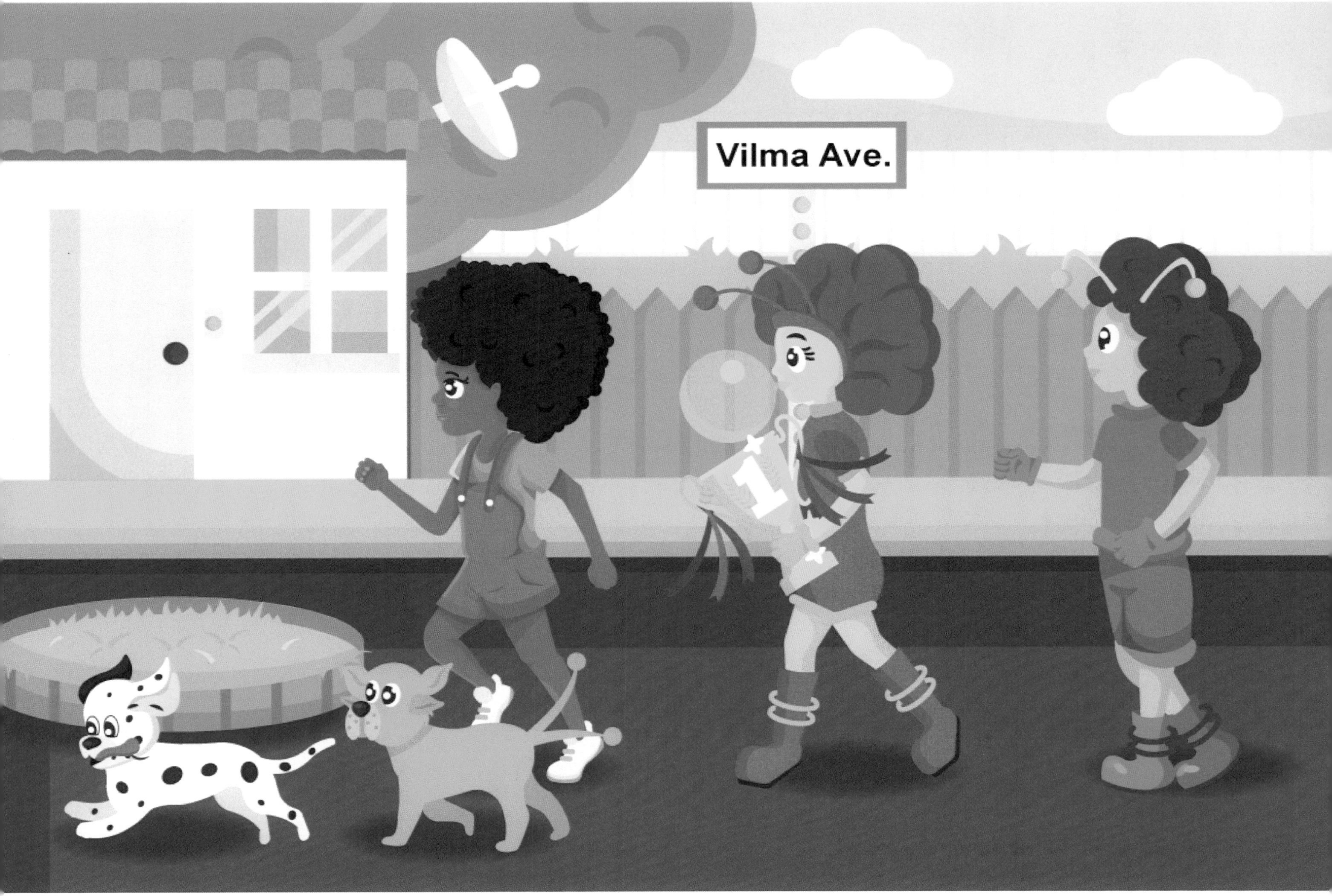
Vilma Ave.

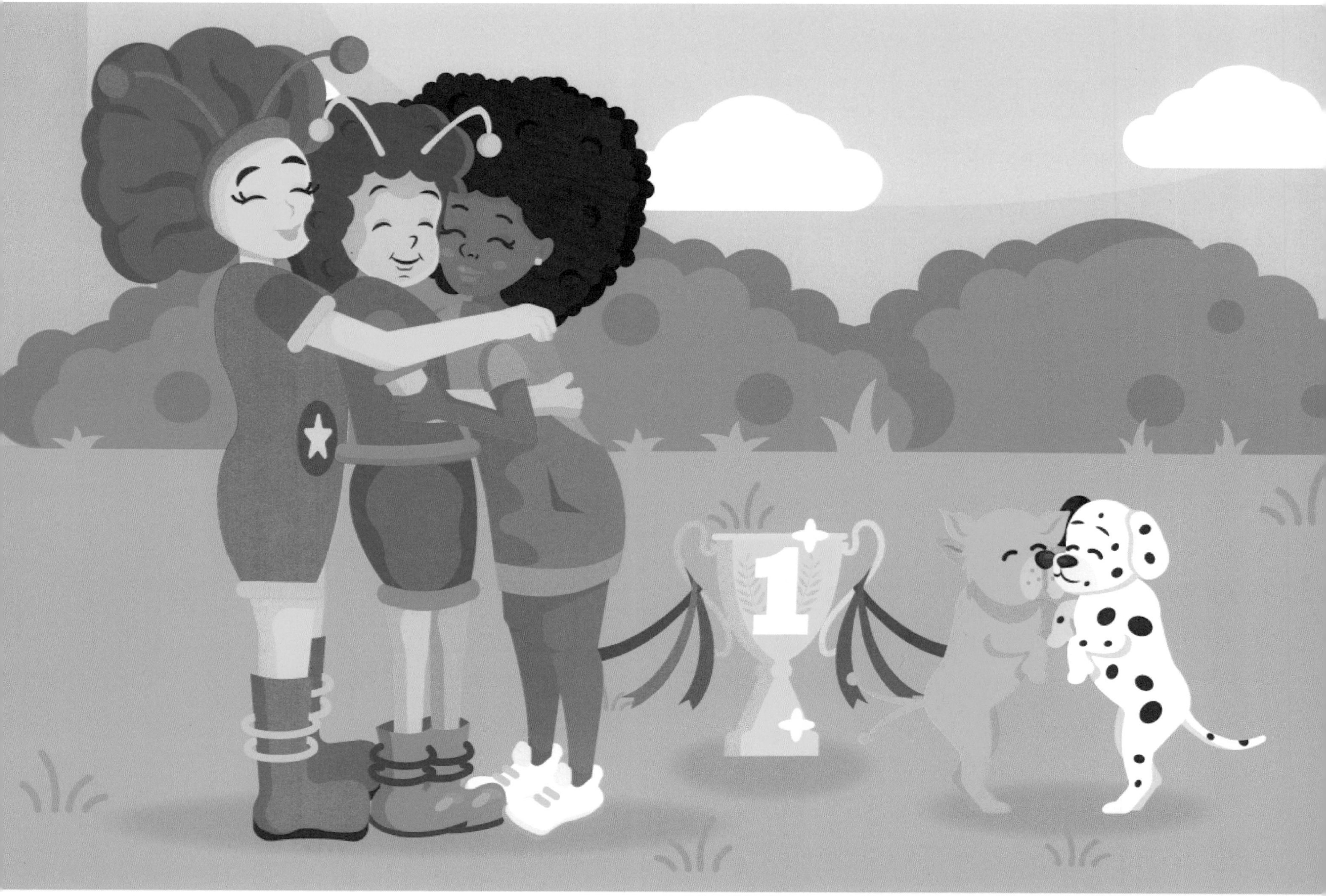
1

Kaley hugs Charlie super tight!

"I will miss you, Charlie!"

Elyot is so happy and overwhelmed. He and Charlie promise each other they will be friends forever. Charlie makes them promise to come back and visit her.

Their dogs rub noses while standing on their hind legs. They also switch places — Seven goes to Europa with Kaley and Elyot, while Nine stays with Charlie.

A bright light appears. Charlie, Kaley, and Seven walk swiftly through the portal and are greeted by their parents and Nik. They cheer for them. Their parents are proud and they put their ribbon up for all to see.

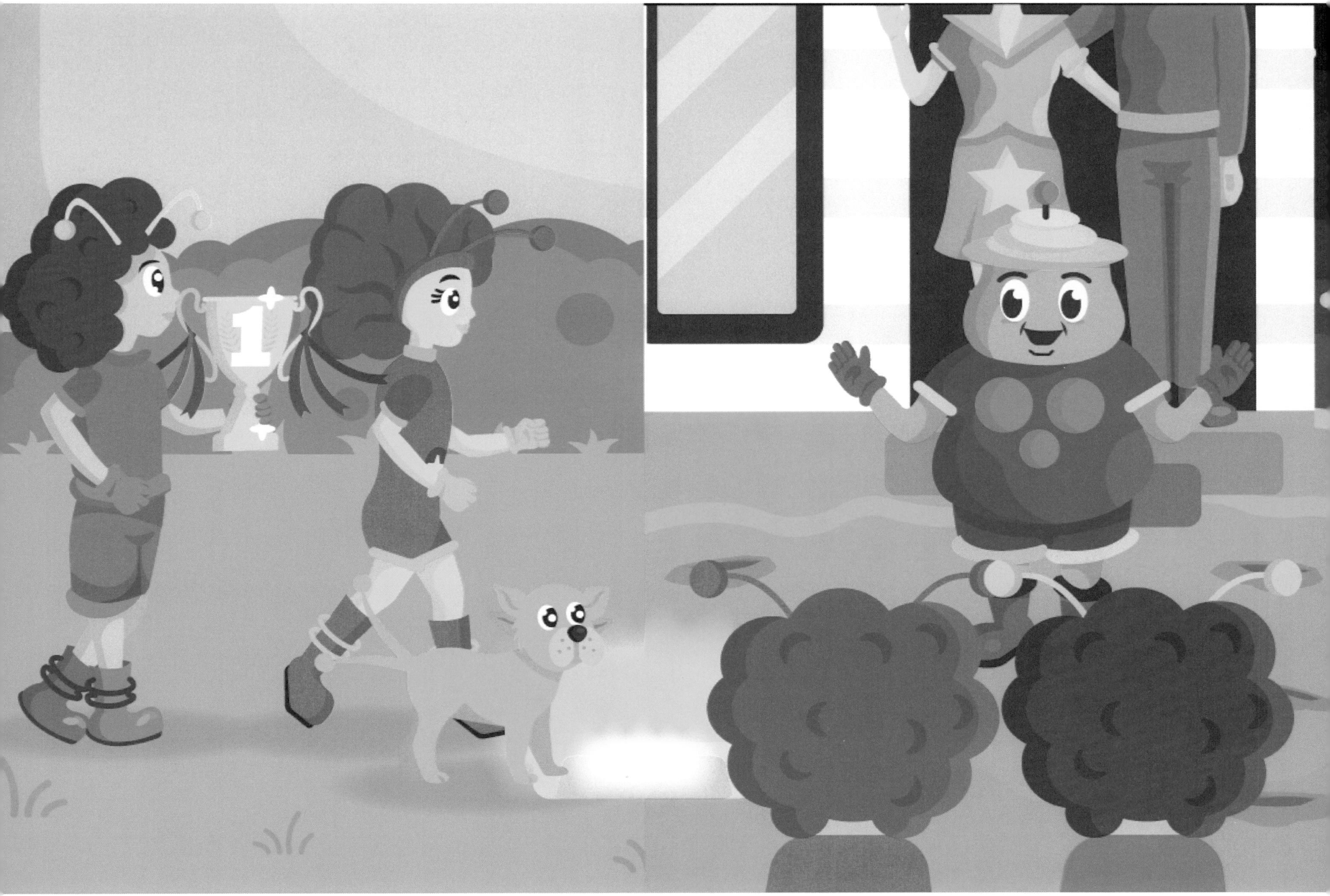
1

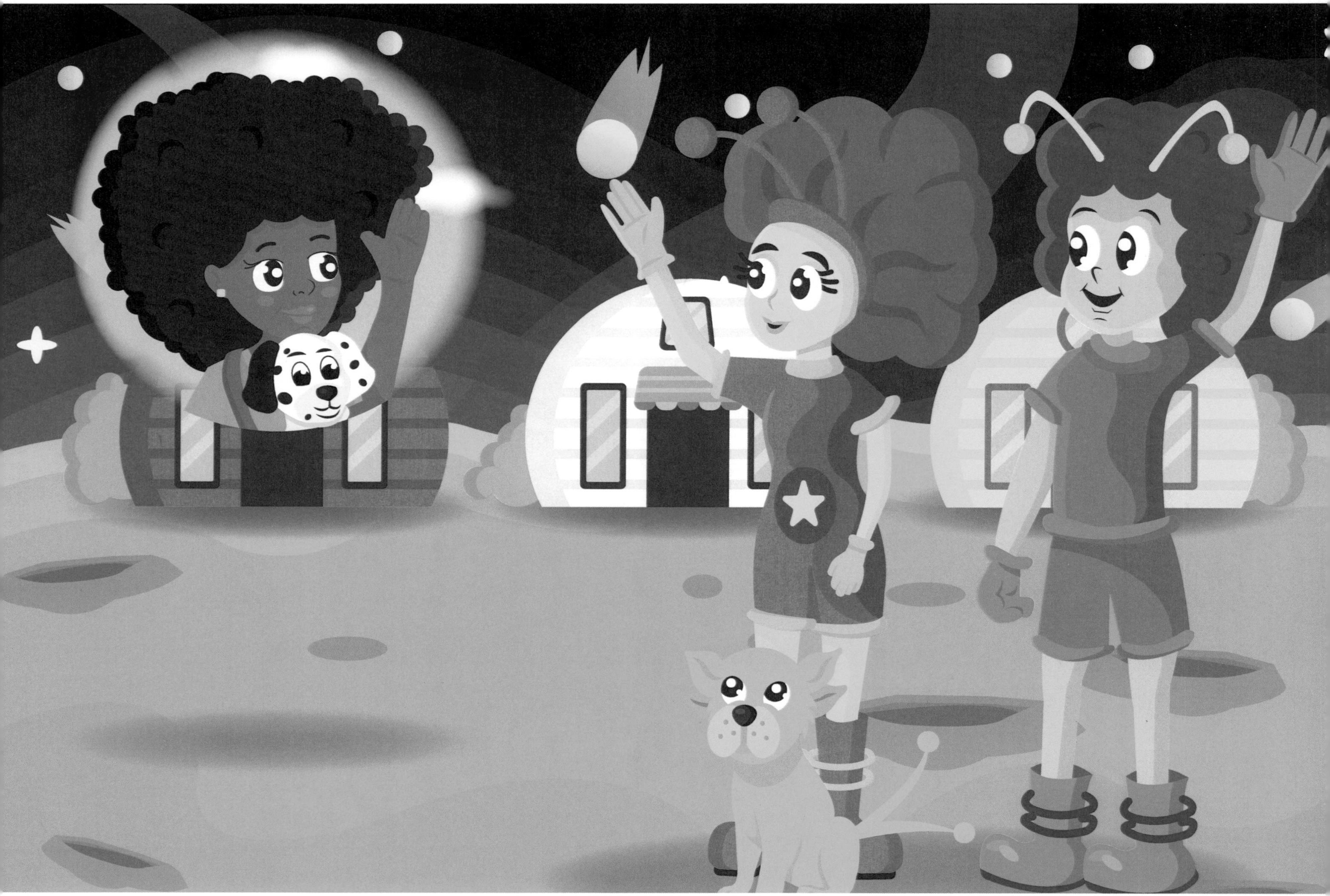

As years go by, they have many adventures and remain only a beam away.

CPSIA information can be obtained
at www.ICGtesting.com
Printed in the USA
LVRC091927021021
699324LV00001B/3

* 9 7 8 1 6 6 2 9 1 2 5 4 2 *